Earth's GROSSEST Animals

Ugly Creatures Under Water

Alix Wood

WINDMILL BOOKS
New York

Published in 2014 by Windmill Books, An Imprint of Rosen Publishing
29 East 21st Street, New York, NY 10010

Editor: Sara Howell
Designer: Alix Wood
Consultant: Sally Morgan

Photo Credits: Cover, 1, 3, 4, 5, 7, 8, 10, 12, 13, 15, 17 left, 18, 19, 20, 21 main, 22, 24, 25, 26, 27 bottom, 28, 29 © Shutterstock; 6 © Birgitte Wilms/Minden Pictures/FLPA; 9 top © Jesper Rautell Balle; 9 bottom © Panela Photo/FLPA; 11 top © Ian Scott/Fotolia; 11 bottom © aconcheng/Fotolia; 14 © Jeff Kubina; 16 © David Evison/Fotolia; 17 right © Jens Petersen; 21 inset © Brocken Inaglory; 23 main © 2004 MBARI; 23 inset © 1999 MBARI; 27 top © Brocken Inaglory.

Library of Congress Cataloging-in-Publication Data

Wood, Alix.
Ugly creatures under water / by Alix Wood.
pages cm. — (Earth's grossest animals)
Includes index.
ISBN 978-1-61533-733-0 (library binding) — ISBN 978-1-61533-783-5 (pbk.) —
ISBN 978-1-61533-784-2 (6-pack)
1. Aquatic animals—Juvenile literature. I. Title.
QL120.W66 2014
591.76—dc23
2012046825

Manufactured in the United States of America

CPSIA Compliance Information: Batch #BS13WM: For Further Information contact Windmill Books, New York, New York at 1-866-478-0556

Contents

What's Hiding in the Water? 4
Weird Walking Fish 6
Creepy Monsters 8
Spiky Creatures 10
Strange Jellyfish 12
Scary Sharks 14
Blobfish and Frogfish 16
Pom-Poms and Horseshoes 18
Underwater Slugs 20
Eight-Armed Creatures 22
Saws and Stings 24
Starfish and Mussels 26
More Strange Crabs 28
Glossary 30
Websites 31
Read More 32
Index 32

What's Hiding in the Water?

There are some really weird creatures living under the water. Some are scary, some are ugly, and some do the strangest things.

Garra rufa fish love to nibble your smelly feet! The garra rufa is sometimes called the doctor fish. They like to gently bite your feet looking for **algae**, and in their search they pick off the dead or diseased skin. Health spas around the world have used garra rufa fish for pedicures, but they can actually spread disease unless the tank is cleaned out between patients.

garra rufa cleaning someone's feet

These little piranhas (right) don't look too scary until you take a look at their teeth!

Piranhas are normally about 5.5 to 10.25 inches (14 to 26 cm) long. They are deadly because they hunt in groups.

Piranhas occasionally bite and sometimes kill people swimming in rivers. In the city of Palmas, Brazil, 190 piranha attacks were reported in the first half of 2007!

When US President Theodore Roosevelt visited the Amazon in 1913, local fishermen showed him how ferocious piranhas are. They blocked off part of the river and starved the piranhas for several days. Then a cow was led into the water and was quickly torn apart by a school of hungry piranhas!

Weird Walking Fish

These two fish could win prizes for looking strange. They wouldn't win prizes for swimming, though. They both prefer to walk!

Like a stealth bomber with lipstick on, the red-lipped batfish is a peculiar looking fish. It is not a good swimmer. Instead it uses its fins to "walk" on the ocean floor.

The batfish has parts on its nose that look like worms. The parts wiggle around to **lure** unsuspecting **prey**.

The devil scorpionfish is hard to spot, half-buried in the ocean floor. They are a dull color similar to the sand or coral on which they live. They are nocturnal, too, which means they are only active at night. Their skin is covered with **venomous** spines and wartlike **glands** which give it a knobbly appearance. Once dug in, it likes to lie still. When it does move, it crawls slowly along the seabed, using its fins.

A devil scorpionfish is a fearsome hunter. When its large mouth opens it creates a **vacuum** which sucks its prey into its mouth!

If it is disturbed by a potential predator, the devil scorpionfish fans out its brilliantly colored fins as a warning.

Creepy Monsters

These underwater creatures have one thing in common. They are funny looking! The axolotl never grows up, and the geoduck grows a little too much for its shell!

"Axolotl" means "water monster." It is an **amphibian**, and a type of salamander, but it never matures into an adult salamander unless forced to do so. Usually a salamander changes from an egg to a larva and finally to adult form. The axolotl stays in its larval form throughout its life.

If an axolotl is made to mature it turns into something resembling this tiger salamander.

The axolotl can regrow its limbs if they are damaged.

The first weird thing about a geoduck (left) is that its name is pronounced "gooey-duck!" It's a large clam that has grown a bit too big for its shell. It buries itself in the sand and can live for up to 160 years in the same place.

The olm is a blind amphibian that lives its life in dark underwater caves. It has adapted to life without light. Because it cannot see, it relies on its sharp hearing and sense of smell. Most amphibians come out of the water at some point, but an olm never does.

The olm is sometimes called the "human fish," because of its pink skin-like color.

Spiky Creatures

You wouldn't want to tread on these spiky underwater animals. They're not just spiky, though. Some are poisonous, too!

A sea urchin (below) can inflict a painful wound if the spines penetrate human skin, but they are not thought to be venomous. Some are very beautiful. A sea urchin moves by using its hundreds of tiny, transparent, sticky "tube feet." Their mouth is underneath them, and their waste comes out the top.

A sea urchin's teeth are self-sharpening. The teeth, which grow continuously, regularly shed damaged areas to keep a sharp cutting edge. A sea urchin's teeth are so sharp it can chew through stone!

A pufferfish is extremely poisonous. Its liver, and sometimes its skin, is highly **toxic** to most animals when eaten. Oddly though, the meat of some species is considered a delicacy in Japan and other parts of Asia. It is prepared by chefs who know which part is safe to eat and in what quantity.

a pufferfish before puffing up its body

A pufferfish is a poor swimmer, but to defend itself it swallows huge amounts of water and turns into a spiky, inedible ball several times its normal size.

a pufferfish puffed up

Strange Jellyfish

Jellyfish look so graceful as they glide along the ocean. They are deadly, though. Jellyfish have tiny stinging cells covering their tentacles that stun or paralyze their prey before they eat them.

Inside a jellyfish's bell-shaped body is its multipurpose mouth. A jellyfish eats and discards waste from the same opening! It also uses the same opening to help it move around. It squirts water from its mouth and the force of this propels it forward. Clever!

The lion's mane jellyfish found in the north Atlantic has a bell which can reach over 6 feet (2 m) across with tentacles as long as 100 feet (33 m)!

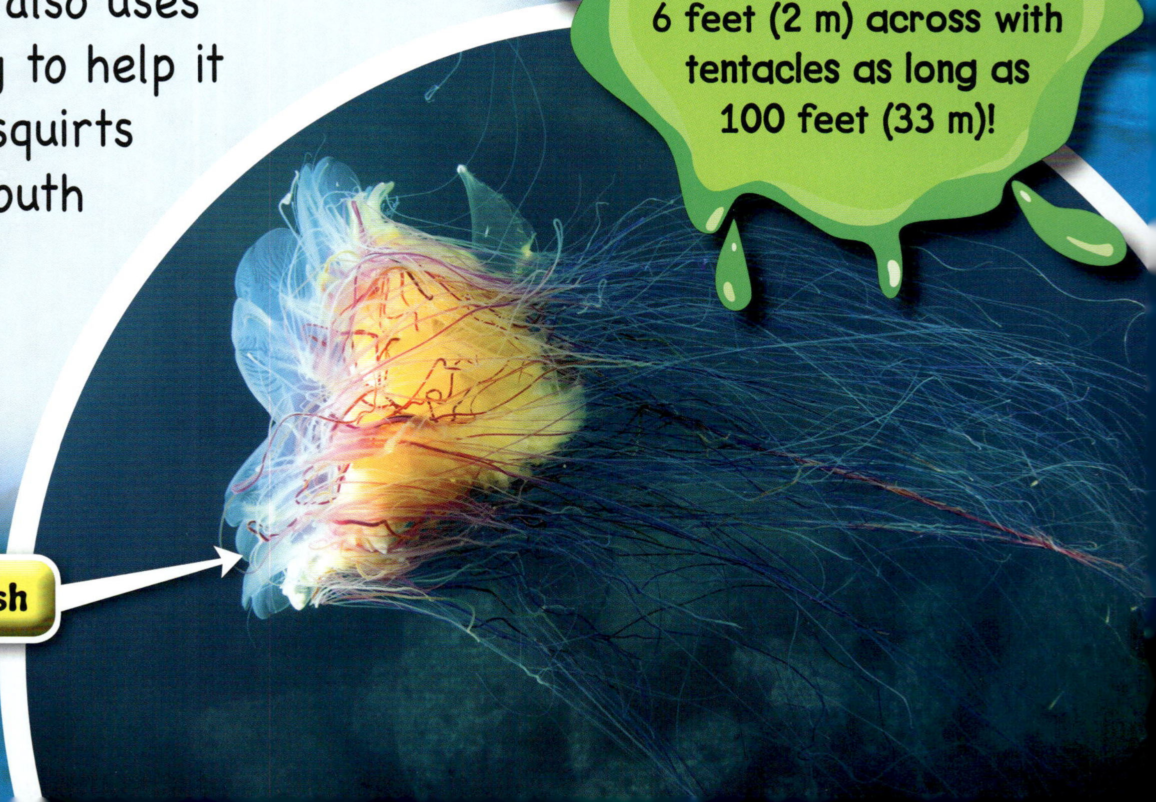

lion's mane jellyfish

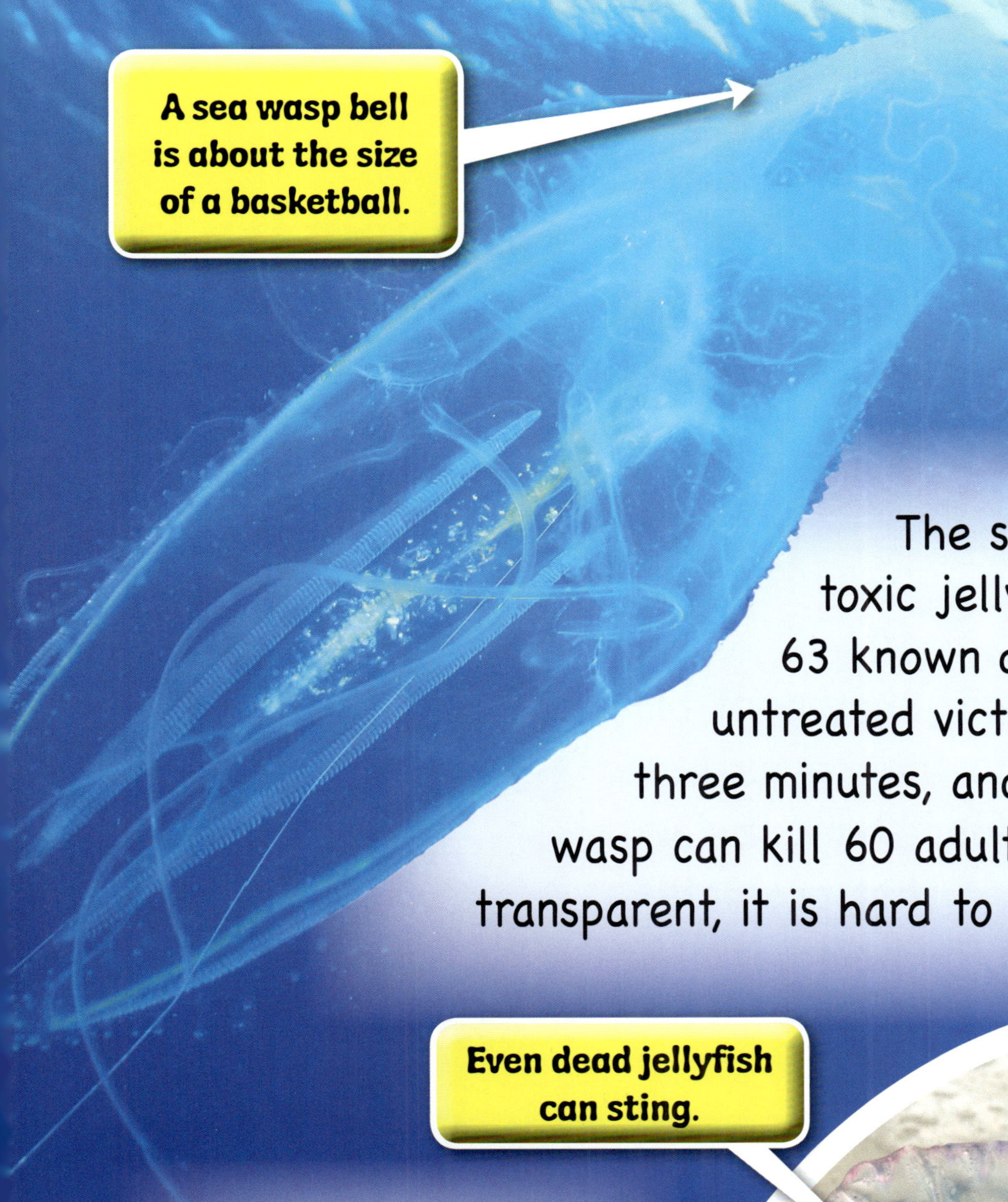

A sea wasp bell is about the size of a basketball.

The sea wasp's pale blue bell has faint markings which, from some angles, look like a skull!

The sea wasp is the most toxic jellyfish, with at least 63 known deaths in Australia. An untreated victim may die in around three minutes, and the venom in one sea wasp can kill 60 adults! Since it is almost transparent, it is hard to spot until it's too late.

Even dead jellyfish can sting.

This poisonous Portuguese man-of-war (right) has a sting as toxic as a cobra's bite.

Scary Sharks

Some sharks can be pretty fierce, although a lot of the large ones just eat tiny shrimp! Sharks are often named after how they look. A hammerhead shark has a head shaped like a hammer, and a whale shark is as big as a whale.

Sharks have eyelids, but they don't blink. They let sea water clean their eyes. Some species like this sand tiger shark (below) have a special **membrane** that protects their eyes while hunting or being attacked.

Sand tiger shark **embryos** eat each other! The largest baby will eat all the others while still growing inside the mother.

A great white shark is the largest predatory fish on Earth. It is fearsome. Its rows of sharp teeth get replaced if it loses any. It has a great sense of smell and organs that can sense tiny **electromagnetic** fields made by its prey.

A great white shark is the only ocean predator to stick its head above the water to look at prey.

A hammerhead shark has an eye on each side of the "hammer," giving it all-around vision. The hammer shape also helps it sense electrical impulses given off by its prey. It swings its head from side to side like a metal detector!

Blobfish and Frogfish

These creatures deserve prizes for both their ugliness and their laziness! They just sit around, waiting for a meal to swim by.

The blobfish lives deep in the ocean. It can survive at such a depth because it is almost entirely made of a gelatin-like substance. This stops the blobfish from sinking as its body is less dense than the sea where it lives.

Blobfish actually have no muscles at all. They really are a blob! They just float around in the same spot waiting for their next meal to go by. Blobfish eat sea urchins and mollusks.

Frogfish are great at hiding, like the giant frogfish below. It looks just like the coral.

Frogfish can be hairy or lumpy. They're often brightly colored to blend in with their coral surroundings. The hairy frogfish (below right) has a wormlike lure which it wiggles around to attract prey. If the frogfish loses its lure, it can grow a new one! In many species the lure can be pulled into a dip in the frogfish's body when it is not needed.

Pom-Poms and Horseshoes

Can you imagine a crab that does an impression of a cheerleader and another that looks like an alien spaceship? These have to be two of the most bizarre things found under water!

This boxer crab (below) is also known as the "pom-pom crab." This weird little crab holds sea anemones in its claws and waves them around if threatened. Sea anemones have stinging tentacles which protect the crab.

The crab uses the anemones as "mops," too! It wipes them along the floor and their sticky tentacles collect small particles of food. Both the crab and the anemone get a good meal, so it suits them both!

Horseshoe crabs are pretty weird, with a body that looks like an armored tank, a scary-looking spiky tail, and ten eyes! They have been around for about 245 million years! They have no jaws. They use their legs to crush their food and move it to their mouth. As a result, they can only eat when they are walking!

If a horseshoe crab gets knocked over by a wave it can die. On land it can't turn itself back over.

Underwater Slugs

There are some plain ugly slug-like creatures under the water. There are some amazingly beautiful ones, too, like the colorful nudibranch.

Nudibranchs are sea snails with no shell. They come in many different shapes and all kinds of bright colors. This should make them easy prey, but the colors are a warning, as most are poisonous.

This brightly colored nudibranch is easy to spot. There is a much shyer fish in the picture, too! See him?

You are what you eat! Some nudibranchs save the chemicals or the stingers from the toxic sponges that they eat and use that as protective poison on their skin!

Sea cucumbers look like a cucumber. That's amazing enough, but they can also **liquefy** their body! Their body wall is made of **collagen**, which can be loosened and tightened at will. If it wants to fit through a small gap, it can loosen its outer skin and squeeze into the space. To keep itself safe once in the crevice, it will hook up all its collagen fibers to make its body firm again!

A sea cucumber eats animal waste and the bodies of dead animals. Despite this, some cultures think sea cucumber is a delicacy!

Some sea cucumbers defend themselves by shooting sticky strands at predators. Some can also discharge a toxic liquid, a little like soap. This can kill any animal nearby.

A sea cucumber ejects sticky filaments in self-defense.

Eight-Armed Creatures

Cuttlefish, squid, and octopuses have a clever smoke screen in store for their unwary predators. They shoot ink out behind them to help cloud the view of predators so they can escape.

A transparent glass squid (left) fills itself with water to seem larger and scarier when threatened. Not only is this squid see-through, but it glows in the dark, too!

a cuttlefish's arms

A cuttlefish hunts by shooting a jet of water to uncover prey buried in the sand. Then it opens its eight arms and shoots out two long, venomous tentacles covered in suckers to grab its prey!

Cuttlefish shoot a brown ink called sepia which was used by the Greeks and Romans as pigment.

The amazingly named vampire squid has webbed skin between its arms which forms an umbrella-shaped net to catch food in. Scientists at the Monterey Bay Aquarium Research Institute, in California, studied its stomach contents and found it eats dead bodies, waste, and mucus!

If threatened, a vampire squid turns its net inside out, exposing fearsome spikes on the underside!

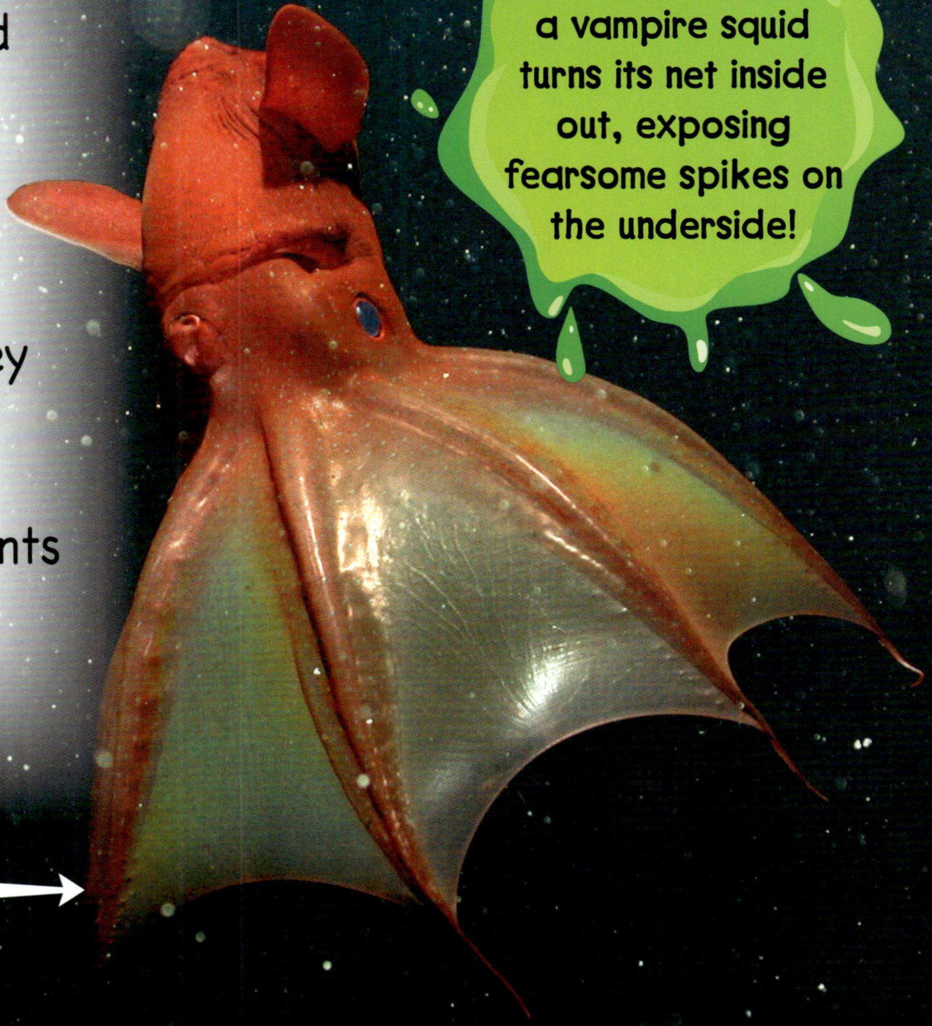

a vampire squid's umbrella-shaped net

The Dumbo octopus (left) has earlike fins that make it look like Walt Disney's flying elephant Dumbo. It lives very deep in the ocean. The largest Dumbo octopus ever recorded was 6 feet (1.8 m) long!

Saws and Stings

Sawfish and stingrays are bizarre-looking creatures. These two types of rays both have strange winglike fins and have their mouths and nostrils on the undersides of their bodies.

A sawfish gets its name from its saw-shaped snout. The saw is covered with sensitive pores that detect moving prey hiding in the seabed. The sawfish uses its saw to dig up buried prey. When fish swim by, the normally lazy sawfish springs from the bottom and slashes at them with its saw. This stuns or injures the prey enough for the sawfish to eat them.

Sawfish sleep in the day and hunt at night. Sawfish do not attack people unless provoked.

Stingrays look as though they are flying through the ocean!

People can get stung if they step on a stingray. To avoid this, shuffle through the water to scare them away.

A stingray has one or more barbed stings on its tail, which it uses for self-defense. The stinger can be 14 inches (35 cm) long, and has two grooves on the underside with venom glands. A stingray usually hides in the sand with just its eyes poking out. Its eyes are on top of its body and its mouth on the underside, so a stingray cannot see its prey. Instead, it has special sensors which detect the tiny electrical charges that the prey emits.

Starfish and Mussels

Mussels really only cause problems because of their numbers. It's a good thing starfish like to eat them!

a life-size blue mussel

Freshwater mussel **larvae** need to live off the body of a fish in order to survive. To get a host fish, a mother mussel waves its wiggling lure. Some emit a smell of rotting flesh to attract scavenger fish. When a fish approaches, the mussel shoots its larvae onto the fish. The larvae attach themselves and live off the fish until they mature.

mussels hitching a ride on a crayfish

Tiny zebra mussels will cling to anything in the water and cause problems by clogging up machinery and harming other underwater creatures.

A starfish eats by attaching to prey and pushing its stomach out through its mouth. **Enzymes** from the starfish's stomach digest the prey. Tiny prey can be swallowed whole.

Light-sensitive eyespots on the tips of its arms help the starfish find food. Favorites on the menu are mollusks such as clams, oysters, and snails.

a starfish eating a mussel

A starfish's arms are covered with tiny pincerlike jaws that keep its skin clear of algae and debris. Suckers help it slowly creep along the ocean floor.

Starfish can grow a new arm if they lose one.

Most starfish have five arms, although some can grow as many as 50 arms.

More Strange Crabs

A hermit crab's shell isn't its own. It's just borrowing it! When a crab gets too big for its shell, it finds an empty one and moves in. Fiddler crabs have one huge, cumbersome claw, and Japanese spider crabs are just huge!

Some hermit crab species use "vacancy chains" to find new shells. When a new, big shell is found, hermit crabs gather around and wait in line from largest to smallest. The largest crab moves in, and then the second biggest crab moves into his old shell, and so on down the line!

Hermit crabs sometimes gang up on another hermit crab that has a great shell. They will actually pry its shell off its back and then fight each other for it!

a hermit crab at home in a snail shell

A male fiddler crab has one claw much larger than the other. It gets in the way when feeding, and it slows the crab down when he is trying to move. However, the male crab needs the big claw to wave in the air to attract a mate! The big claw also helps cool the crab down, as it transfers heat from the body to the claw. This means male fiddler crabs can stay on the surface longer, looking for food and waving!

Japanese spider crabs' big claws have been known to cause injuries, but the crabs mainly eat fish that are already dead.

Japanese spider crabs can have a leg span up to about 13 feet (4 m).

Glossary

algae (AL-jee)
Plantlike lifeforms that mostly grow in water.

amphibian (am-FIH-bee-un)
An animal able to live both on land and in water.

collagen (KAH-luh-jin)
A protein found in connective tissue.

delicacy (DEH-lih-kuh-see)
Something pleasing to eat because it is rare or a luxury.

electromagnetic (ih-lek-troh-mag-NEH-tik)
Magnetism developed by a current of electricity.

enzymes (EN-zymz)
Complex proteins produced by living cells.

glands (GLANDZ)
Organs that make and secrete saliva, sweat, or bile from a plant or animal body.

larvae (LAHR-vee)
An early form of animal that at birth or hatching is very different from its parents.

liquefy (LIH-kwuh-fy)
To make or become liquid.

lure (LUR)
A decoy for attracting animals to capture.

membrane (MEM-brayn)
A thin, soft, flexible layer.

predator (PREH-duh-ter)
An animal that lives by killing and eating other animals.

prey (PRAY)
An animal hunted or killed by another animal for food.

tentacles (TEN-tih-kulz)
Long, flexible armlike body parts used for feeling or grasping.

toxic (TOK-sik)
Of a poisonous substance produced by a living organism that is poisonous to other organisms.

vacuum (VA-kyoom)
A space from which most of the air has been removed.

venomous (VEH-nuh-mis)
Having or producing poison.

WEBSITES

For web resources related to the subject of this book, go to: www.windmillbooks.com/weblinks and select this book's title.

Read More

Metz, Lorijo. *Discovering Starfish*. Along the Shore. New York: PowerKids Press, 2012.

Roza, Greg. *Poke!: The Sea Urchin and Other Animals with Spikes*. Armed and Dangerous. New York: PowerKids Press, 2011.

Sullivan, Jody. *Crabs*. Under the Sea. Mankato, MN: Capstone Press, 2006.

Index

A
axolotl 8

B
blobfish 16
boxer crab 18

C
crabs 18, 19, 28, 29
cuttlefish 22

D
devil scorpionfish 7
Dumbo octopus 23

F
fiddler crab 28, 29
frogfish 16, 17

G
garra rufa fish 4
geoduck 8, 9
glass squid 22
great white shark 15

H
hammerhead shark 14, 15
horseshoe crabs 19

J
jellyfish 12, 13

M
mussels 26, 27

N
nudibranchs 20

O
olm 9

P
piranhas 5
pufferfish 11

R
red-lipped batfish 6

S
sand tiger shark 14
sawfish 24
sea anemones 18
sea cucumbers 21
sea urchins 10, 16
sea wasps 13
starfish 26, 27
stingray 24, 25